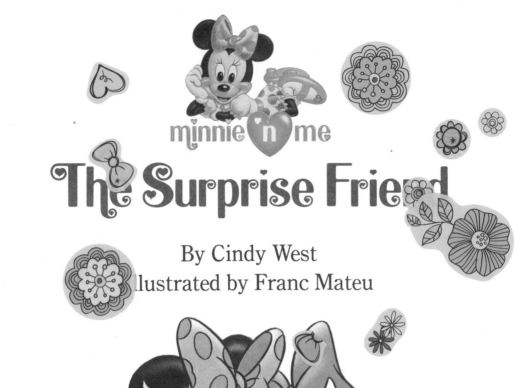

minnie 'n me
The Surprise Friend

By Cindy West
Illustrated by Franc Mateu

A Golden Book • New York
Western Publishing Company, Inc., Racine, Wisconsin 53404

Daisy calls to Minnie.
"Come with me,"
she says.
"Help me find
a big surprise."

"Who is the surprise for?"
Minnie asks.

"It is for a good friend,"
says Daisy.

"Look at this!"
says Daisy.
"Do you like it,
Minnie?"
"Yes," says Minnie.
"I think so."
"I do not!" says Daisy.

7

"Look at this!"
says Daisy.
"Do you like it,
Minnie?"

"No!"
says Minnie.
"I do not like it!"

"Look at this!"
says Daisy.
"Will your friend
like that?"
asks Minnie.

"I do not know,"
says Daisy.
"Do YOU like it?"
"Yes," says Minnie.

"This is very nice, too,"
says Minnie.
"Do you like it
more than that?"
asks Daisy.
"Oh, yes, Daisy!"
says Minnie.

"Will your friend
like this?"
asks Minnie.
"No," says Daisy.
"It is too big for her."

"Daisy," says Minnie.
"Who is your good friend?
Do you like her
more than me?"
Daisy will not tell.

"It is hard
to help you,"
Minnie says.
"Yes, it is," says Daisy.
"You may as well go."
"I WILL!" says Minnie.
"Good-bye!"

Two days go by.
Penny and Daisy come
to Minnie's house.
Other friends come, too.

"Happy birthday!"
they all shout.
"Happy birthday, Minnie!"

They all play.

They all sing.

They all eat cake.

"Open this first!"
Daisy says.

"Oh!" Minnie cries.
"This is the book
I like!"

"Yes!" Daisy says.
"Surprise!
YOU are my very good friend!
You are my BEST friend!"

"I AM!" Minnie says.
"I am so happy!"

"I am happy, too!"
says Daisy.
And Minnie writes all about it
in her new book.